St Marys

Richard Toward

This is a work of fiction

Any resemblance to persons living or dead, is entirely coincidental.

Printed in UK by Donkeydick press Ltd

First paperback edition Dec 2013

Newcastle

Book design David Morrison

ISBN: 978-1-291-64397-8

For KERRIE (R.I.P)

STUART

ELOISE

CHRISTOPHER

The children who inspired then went on and had children

Of their own.

Acknowledgements and a million thank yous to;

Denny Toward. The cleverest woman I have ever met who put up with me Love ya loads.

Michael Riddell. Author.

To you the reader, who has taken the time to view what I have written.

I was sad, dunno why, just was. The only way I can describe it is kinda like a dark cloud had descended over my head and decided to piss on me continuously. My body felt heavy and my breathing laboured. I wanted to cry but no tears would come.

So maybe I do talk to myself, I think I make perfectly good sense.

I am sharp and observant and my talking harms no one. I make the judgements and choose my words carefully. Methodically.

Sorry did you think I was talking to you?

Of course there is a fucking God. Well if there wasn't one then we would have to just invent one because we have to believe in something. There has to be more. This can't be the end… yet.

I am lying in my room at 7am listening to the bin men emptying the bins.

My Uncle Theodore was very tall and yet thin and gaunt with a grey sallow face and prematurely grey hair. He certainly didn't look like a man in the best of health. I didn't even know I had an uncle until he turned up on the doorstep a few days before my fifteenth birthday. It was raining. Huge droplets that scoured the ground and rapped noisily on windows and amidst this stood a tall man with a black umbrella and a matching long coat that went down to his knees. He actually looked like he was going to, or had just been, to a funeral. He closed his umbrella and gave it a brisk shake then actually pushed past me to stand dripping in the hall. It was only then he spoken "Hello Luke I am pleased to meet you eventually." His smile was warm and reassuring and he held out his thin hand. I am your uncle Theodore". I took his wet hand rather speechless and more than a little confused. I wiped my hand on my trousers.

The sitting room door opened and my father appeared with my mother, as always behind him. He stopped dead mid stride and momma bumped into him. They stood staring like they had seen a ghost and my dad's face paled noticeably.

After a hesitant pause that was embarrassing in its length, father smiled broadly to reveal his white even, mostly false, teeth and mother took her cupped hands from her mouth. "Luke will you take your uncles wet coat and hang it up." It was heavy and I had to hold it high to stop it trailing along the floor after it was handed to me unceremoniously by my new found uncle and I took it to the cupboard.

After much backslapping and handshaking, hugging and cheek kissing they settled in the living room for a coffee. I gathered he was my father's older brother who had been travelling the world. It was getting late and they wanted to talk adult talk and I was duly sent to bed.

OH DEAR

She was so beautiful in life. A true classic beauty loved by all and gazed upon with envious eyes by women. A vision to behold.

She was beautiful in death. A serene pale face, full ruby red lips, long curling lashes and perfectly plucked eyebrows.

Poor Snow White never knew what hit her when she took a bite of that enchanted rosy red apple.

My new Uncle Theodore rented a small bungalow with a large unkempt garden about half a *mile or so from my parents' house. He used to spend some time around our house and kept inviting me around to have a look at his crib, as he called it. One day I took him up on it and called round after school. Initially I was a bit hesitant and nervous of my new found uncle. Although he was around my house regularly, I really had very little to do with him. He spent most of the time with my dad. (It was my dad who had persuaded me to visit Uncs bungalow). My uncle Theodore was dressed all in white with a shirt, trousers and slip on trainers when he finally opened the door on my third knock, he did look smart. The fresh Northumberland air had done him the power of good and he had gradually, over the past few weeks lost the grey sickly look he had at our first meeting. He made tea and cream scones with strawberry jam. I remember it well and it was the first of many. I got into a routine of going to his house straight from school on Fridays and he helped with my homework after tea then I would head for home.*

My mam and dad are teachers and they made it plain that I was a mistake. They kinda left me to my own devices and as long as I attended school and got good grades they didn't really bother with me apart from mealtimes when they had to talk. They worked at my school but fortunately didn't take any of my lessons. At home I spent most of my time in my large bedroom watching TV or reading. The library was my best friend.

THE PERFECT WIFE

It was mid-November, and the chill wind nips but rarely bites at this time of year. Heavy rain laden clouds glided across a dark grey sky as though sombrely awaiting a catastrophic event.

Sarah Kennedy wandered around her house aimlessly, bored. She took in the expensive velvet curtains, Persian hand made carpets and the carefully chosen antiques that complemented her furniture.

She had married well.

Sarah remembered the home she had lived in as a child. A small two bedroomed with coats on the bed and the constant smell of fried food and cigarette smoke. They were poor but mother made sure they never went hungry. She remembered going to the outside toilet in the yard during the night. Freezing cold, chattering teeth and seeing the eyes of malevolent cats watching her intently from the top of the yard walls.

Sarah Kennedy was pretty, exceptionally pretty, with eyes bluer than the deep tranquil lakes of Ireland, shoulder length ash blonde hair worn at the moment in a high ponytail, unblemishished skin like porcelain. Sarah hadn't clawed or worked her way to the way to the top of the tree, she had simply used her looks to marry well. Her husband was fifteen years her senior and a renowned scientist. They had met while she was working as a chambermaid and he was staying in the Brighton hotel for a weekend. He was attending a scientific sharing ideas conference. It was a yearly gathering by invitation only and they had met in its third year. Two years on and they had married and he had gone to the convention again. He had only been away a couple hours and she was already bored. Sarah could have went with him, she did last year. Brighton was a long way to travel though by rail and taxi from Newcastle, especially when she was seven months pregnant and she also had an ulterior motive for staying at home.

She wanted to see his room. His secret room where he spent many hours after work. His private sanctuary from the outside world and Sarah was not allowed in.

He had lived here in Darras Hall for ten years and Sarah had moved into his modern luxury house and after three idyllic months they married. His name by the way, is John. John George Kennedy, you may have heard of him? He had this private room before he met Sarah and he kept it on during their marriage. He would spend an hour in there in the morning before work and two or more hours there on an evening. Every evening. Possibly more if he could. Then Sarah started to question her husband about the room.

"What is in there?" was her first question.

"Why can't I go in.?" was her second. She asked them many times in many ways. At first John replied that it was just his own private room where he tried out several scientific ideas not relating to work. Work being at Cramlington pharmaceuticals in the production of drugs for asthma and prostate cancer. If Sarah pushed him more, John would become agitated and say "it's too dangerous, very dangerous, it's a fully functional science room so just stop asking because it isn't going to happen." They didn't really argue but John raised his voice when she questioned him about his room.

"The room is a very dangerous place for those who don't know it hun. Just stop asking okay and one day when you are least expecting it, I will take you in and show you around."

Sarah had stopped asking. But it was only to be the calm before the storm and she schemed and planned to see it by one means or another.

The door was situated at the back of the house at the end of a long corridor with one painting on the wall to break up the bland stark whiteness of the corridor. Two autumnal trees in a pale green field against the setting sun. The door was large and very wide and made of solid pine. Old unvarnished solid pine that was out of place in this modern luxury house. A plain brass doorknob faded with time and in need of a good polish sat above the lock; watching it like a sentinel.

But now she wanted to see inside more than ever. John had explained that he was having the key lock changed to a fingerprint recognition lock and would have to call in a specialist but it would have to wait until he got back from the conference.

It had to be now or she would always be wondering.

Sarah managed to get the key by waiting until he was asleep and snoring loudly. (She had seen this in a movie). Pressing the key into some plastercine making sure it got into all the grooves and furrows to make a cast. (She had saw the movie twice). During the day he wore the key around his neck but it went into his trouser pocket at night. It was the longest moment of her life. Her breathing was laboured and she was visibly perspiring. Mission accomplished.

A locksmith made the key from the cast and got something extra for his troubles and for asking no questions. Sarah being so pretty and a little flirtatious with him maybe helped in swaying his judgement. She hid the key in her knicker drawer.

She took a deep breath and took the first step down the corridor, the large pine door seemed larger and more imposing with each tentative step. She paused at the large picture on the wall that could only be looked at directly from this area of the hallway. She stared. There was something standing between the trees. Human and yet different in many ways. A something, not a someone. It was indistinct though and could have just been a shadow with one hand resting on a tree, but it looked alive and out of place in the picture. She had never noticed it before. Sarah turned back to the door and sighed. A chill ran down her spine and she would have turned back but it was too late. There was no way she could retrace her steps, she had come too far.

The key slipped in the lock and turned with a loud clunk but it took her a couple seconds before she plucked up the courage to turn the knob. Sarah Kennedy stepped in. The room was bathed in a blue light and she moved in another step. To her right she noticed an alarm panel with numbers and took another step beyond the electronic panel. Something caught her eye near the back of the large room. Something had moved. Another step.

Sarah heard the angry crackle of the laser before she saw the thin yellow beam hotter than the surface of the sun. Her darting eyes took in the metal posts around the walls, floor and ceiling before the laser cut her into four. . Through muscle sinew and bone, cauterising as it sliced. . Her beautiful blue eyes almost bulged out of their sockets yet strangely she felt no pain but realised her life and that of her child had ended. A tear slid down her cheek. Her baby was going to be a girl. They had even chose her name. Thick blood bubbled from her lips.

Something watched her from the shadows with fiery red unblinking eyes. Watched her like a hungry lion would watch its prey. It stirred.

The laser was also meant to keep things in.

She had been warned; had been told a hundred times.

His laboratory was a very dangerous place. John had explained had told her and had even raised his voice at Sarah but…curiosity killed the cat.

One Friday I stayed over at Uncle Theodore's. My parents agreed to it a bit too hastily for my liking while marking test papers in the dining room. They always took their work home at the weekends. I changed out of my school uniform and walked to Uncs house on a warm evening with a low sun. As I approached his door the sky darkened and thunder roared. The threatened rain didn't fall though until I was in his house sipping on a coke. After a fish and chip supper he said "Tonight I am going to tell you a true story. But first we must set the mood young sky walker." We lit several candles and turned out the lights.

THE WEDDING

The vicarage of Walkerdene in Northumberland was a rather grand house, built in 1855, of warm orange marmalade coloured bricks and pan tiles. The large house bulged forward with two curved bays with the huge windows superseded into smaller white framed panels. They looked out onto a gravelled driveway and over a manicured lawn. The grey sombre church was connected to the house via a stone hallway.

There was much hustle and bustle about the house today. There were numerous deliveries and esteemed guests arriving. Flowers, decorations, food, dresses and suits tailored from the finest satins and silks were being delivered.

Today the daughter of Vicar Arthur Kendall was to be married.

Being a vicar's daughter was a heavy burden Anne had shouldered all her life and it was no easier to bear because of its familiarity. She was expected to behave as though it were a family business that she would one day inherit. There was more good and kindness in Anne as not so when any ill will or thought entered her head, then a quick prayer and the thought would be banished to a dark distant corner of her mind. Goodness always prevailed on Anne's slim shoulders and the devil never rested long on them.

Folk were coming from far and wide to attend the wedding. Her father Arthur was a renowned vicar whose passionate sermons many travelled great distances to hear. His daughter was known for her perfect skin and blonde ringlets. She never had a bad word to say about anyone and her beautiful smile lit up a room.

The wedding went off perfectly.

The feasting saw many gluttons.

The dancing saw few sloths.

Her long white dress many envied.

Before the grand opening of the presents they played games as was traditional in the 1800s.

"The bride must choose the first game", announced Vicar Kendall, puffing out his chest with a pride that could not be contained. His only child had married a fine kind man, who was a good Christian from a wealthy family of land owners.

"Blind man's bluff", yelled one guest.

"Skittles" shouted another.

"Racing." Yelled a very fat man who obviously couldn't run.

"Ssshhh let the bride decide", said the vicar in an authorative voice.

Anne's smile broadened. "How about Hide and Seek? My new hubby and I will hide in different places of course and you have to find us." The hundred or so guests murmured agreement. Anne loved Walkerdene House and knew it well, it was going to be her first obvious choice.

Reverend Kendall watched as his daughter and her new husband went out of the door to hide. He never saw her again.

One can only imagine the confusion and then despair of the wedding party and her father, the compassionate reverend Kendall, who searched the house every day until his death. He died a couple years later, they say of a broken heart. I also think that he did, his sorrow and pain must have been unbearable.

Then bout ten years ago there was a big renovation project on the house and church with scaffolding and building work being undertaken.

Along the passage from house to church there was a secret door and several steps that led down in a spiral to a store room beneath the church. It was discovered accidentally. Two workmen, a plasterer and a joiner entered the hidden room tentatively. There was a dusty chair and a desk and in the corner a heavy oak blanket chest. The big lock had clicked shut and locked in poor Anne Kendall on her wedding day. The rusted lock and wood groaned with dismay at being jemmied open and with a loud crack, it revealed its secret.

Anne, still in her wedding dress, knees drawn up, her mummified face staring at them. Her hands, fingers interlocked as though still in prayer. Her lips pulled back to reveal her teeth. The eyes were gone but the face stared accusingly at them. Bill Fry the foreman on the job, and his companion stared back at Anne. Just stood and stared unable to find their voices. After what seemed an age Bill Fry looked up at the inside of the oak lid to see it smeared with blood. Poor Anne. How long before she realised she couldn't be found? How many days sleeping, waking, muscle cramps starving, thirsty all in pitch black darkness always the darkness. The screams and cries unheard.

Bill Fry tore himself away from what was her coffin, the image of her imprinted into his brain and he spent many nights too afraid to sleep lest the corpse wake up and chase him. With a heavy heart and trembling legs he went over to the desk and noticed some papers which he shook the dust from and used his finger to brush them clean. He read through the last couple of scrawled lines with shock and horror.

"Tomorrow I am to be wed to the most wonderful man but he does not yet know I am bearing his child. I am so happy."

Next to the papers was the key to fit the blanket box. The lock hadn't clicked shut, it had been locked.

I was silent.

My uncle Theodore leaned back in his armchair. "That's a true story young Luke skywalker. Consider this when you go to sleep. Bill Fry spent some months in a mental institution after that. He thought the ghost of the pregnant Anne Kennedy was haunting him for disturbing her forced sleep." He stood up stiffly. "I'll make us a mug of hot chocolate I got some whipped cream and chocolate sprinkles".

That night I had very little sleep.

The summer holidays were coming up. No school for six weeks. My mam and dad always took me to Blackpool for a week and Benidorm for six days during the holidays. Same every year. I approached the subject with my father head on, no beating about the bush. He preferred questions done that way. "I want to stay with Uncle Theodore during the school holidays. I don't want to go on holiday or abroad. I have fifteen years of catching up with an uncle I never even knew I had. He tells such fantastic stories dad and I can help him sort out the garden".

My dad nodded his head slowly, thoughtfully. " I will speak to Theodore first and then your mother."

"I have mentioned it to Uncs and he said it was up to you."

"Nevertheless I will still speak to him and your mam." He liked to have the final say in most things relating to the family so his talk would be a lecture.

I walked away with a wry smile. This year they could have a holiday where they wanted while I spent a few weeks with my long lost Uncle.

His stories are always true (he said). They are told as a matter of fact, without any embellishment or regalia. They enthralled me and I needed to hear more.

AGE

I am an old man now, older than most men my age. Still have my hair cept it's turned white and on my chest. Just up and jumped offa my head one night to rest on the pillow. Then reappeared a few years later, thick and black. It was on my shoulders and then spread like creeping tendrils out of my nose and ears and down my back to places I can't reach anymore. Then all the colour left it. The piggent I think it is called. Well all the piggent left it and it went from black to white, with no grey tween.

I believe I had a wife once, maybe two. One was called Ladbrokes.

"Mary, Mary, quite contrary what days it? What month? What year?

I have heard the word altzeimers mentioned in several conversations. Was my wife called Marilyn? Think I had children too but can't put a name to the faces.

Sometimes I am aware that huge tracts of my memory have gone, slipping away, out of my reach. Familiar and even beloved faces have all silently melted from my head and my heart. Their names are gone along with the memories of them. Dead to me, although they still lived. I pray for death every night, at least I think I do; hope I do. If god is so benevolent and kind why is he doing this to me? I was a good man. Most times I can't even remember my own name now. My memory is failing. I still have hair…

I think I will go to sleep now. Am sure things will be better in the morning.

THE CHRISTIAN

"When will I get to see Jesus mammy?"

Jessica Hartnell sighed heavily and clenched her teeth together.

"Mammy?"

"I hope it will be a very long time before you see him. I have already explained that a person has to die before they can see him. Daddy and I…"

"I want to see him now!" Mrs Jones says that we all will get to see him if we are kind and good. I am good aren't I mammy?"

"Jessica looked down at her daughter. "Yes of course you are. Sometimes you are too good to be true. I do wish occasionally that you would misbehave."

"Oh but I couldn't do that, because then Jesus wouldn't come to see me" There was hurt in the seven year olds eyes.

Carol followed her mother into the kitchen and watched with mild interest as she filled the sink with hot water and washing up liquid. She placed the dirty dishes that were on the bench into the mass of bubbles.

"You have to die hun before he will take your hand and before that you will have grown up, probably married and have children of your own." Jessica placed a red rose flowered cup onto the draining board and looked down at her only child noticing, as though for the very first time, how pretty and cherubic her face appeared, surrounded as it was by shoulder length mousey brown hair. "One day when you are least expecting it he will come down and only then take your hand and lead you into heaven. Just stop going on about it hun okay." Although Jessica spoke calmly and softly her dark eyes were troubled.

Carol stroked her chin thoughtfully before saying "I can't wait year's mammy I want to see him now,"

Her father entered the kitchen with a newspaper under his arm, silently in his black suede well-worn carpet slippers. "She isn't still going on about this religious lark." It was more a statement than a question and it didn't need to be answered. He continued briskly,

“Ever since they have taught her about Jesus at school she has never stopped going on about it. Can’t believe they still fill their heads with such nonsense.”

“Leave her alone Dave, it’s just a phase she will grow out of it soon enough.”

“Well she has been going through this phase now for nearly four months and am really just sick of it. Its time I put an end to this nonsense once and for all.”

“Go and play next door with Elaine babe. You can have a look at some of the presents she got for her birthday last week.” Jessica ushered her daughter towards the kitchen door. “Me and your daddy need a private word. “ She leaned forward and kissed her seven year old on the top of her head. “Go on it’s a lovely day and the sun is shining.” She smiled a fake smile and then waited for the argument.

“She needs to see a child psychiatrist. A story shouldn’t affect a child so much.” Dave said then he held his hand up defensively as Jessica turned on him with blazing eyes. “Just hold on okay just humour me for a minute. “ Dave raised his voice “There is something wrong with her okay.” He changed the subject before his wife could reply. “Is this Mrs Haynes some kind of religious nut?”

His wife took the bait. “Don’t be stupid Dave, it’s just school policy to teach religious education to all the pupils. Saint Josephs is a catholic school with several nuns as teachers.”

“But what if I don’t want her learning anymore about God and Jesus for now. She is very trusting and impressionable at her age. “

“Yes but she is top of the class in all her subjects which shows she is very bright.”

“But I can’t understand this weird obsession she has with Jesus.”

Jessica smiled and said. “She is perfectly perfect in every way borne of our love for one another. Maybe she is an angel who has lost her way.” She stepped forward to kiss her husband.

A loud scream followed by the screeching of a car froze her husband’s reply and smile into a rictus grin. For what seemed like hours they stood like goose peppered statues, afraid to move, afraid to even think.

Jessica's eyes widened and her voice was trembling "Oh dear God no." her hand reached up to cover her mouth.

The spell was broken. Dave turned and ran through the door and along the path giving an anguished cry as he saw a small crowd gathering in the centre of the road. Like grim reapers descending upon a dying soul. He elbowed his way through the hunched shoulders his ears deaf to the whispers of "poor child" and "mustn't have seen him coming".

The hushed muttering died as neighbours realised the dad was here now. The nightmare that had troubled all caring parents throughout time was now a reality for David and Jessica Hartnell. Their lives would never be the same again.

It was Carol. She lay on her side with a large bruise on her face that was touching the pavement. Dave got on the ground and gently eased her onto her back with her head resting on his leg. There was a little blood coming from her nose and mouth. Her eyes flickered open, recognition came quickly because there was no pain. She spoke in a hoarse whisper. "I couldn't ...couldn't wait years...and year's daddy, I just...couldn't." Then her eyes closed for the last time and Jesus took her hand.

Then somewhere behind him he heard Jessica begin to scream and it seemed to last an eternity.

My Uncle Theodore took me to museums and libraries and movies during the school holidays. It was the best six weeks I have ever had in my life. Every day something new, different and exciting. Father occasionally happened by and although he always gave me some money I resented him coming. He never stayed long, usually less than an hour but it felt to me like he was intruding and spying on our own little world.

My Uncle and I weeded the garden which had blossomed beautifully. A Perfectly cut lawn bordered by flowering plants and a tyre painted white as a centrepiece holding a white and blue floral arrangement in full bloom.

The First World War was fought by men and boys in muddy trenches.

The Second World War was fought by men and machines.

The Third world war was fought by men pushing red buttons.

The fourth world war was fought by men with spears and knives.

"Perhaps I should not be telling you these stories", my Uncle said later that evening over the supper table. "They could give you nightmares Luke."

"I am only here for your stories. You sound like my dad now, that's the kind of thing he would say. Looking after my welfare he called it. I can make my own mistakes they do say you should learn by them and I am fifteen. Father is fine if I am in my room and reading or studying but when I want to go out into the street he gets kind of worried and agitated."

"Perhaps he has his reasons" Uncle Theodore said. "They will become apparent when you reach of age. That is all I can say on that subject at this moment." Unc leaned forward and picked up the beautiful hand painted teapot of a mountain scene. He had acquired it in a small Northern town in China called Fusong in a quaint bargain basement shop and haggled with the owner over the price. "More tea Luke?"

"Yes please," I said and slid my cup across.

WHERE IS THY STING?

Not too long ago a young man died. He was very sick and he knew he was going to die so he gave his possessions away as his body got ready for the journey. His mind was strong however and he fought against death using technology and powerful medications.

The illness took hold slowly and death never to be dismayed, played out the battle.

He turned a strong will into a weak and sickly mind. The young man became bed ridden and could not clean himself nor feed himself.

It was a sad lingering death with no real quality of life.

Perhaps there is something to be said for a quick end to life. A sudden unexpected death.

When it comes to you do not fight it just give in gracefully and death will come quicker and be more merciful.

THE CRACK

My flat is small and pokey and I just love it because it is mine. All mine.

After a messy divorce and a child I don't see anymore, although I pay high maintenance, it is all I can afford after I gave the bitch the house and all the contents I had worked so many years for.

It was only after I had moved in that I noticed the small crack in the ceiling. I was lying in bed on my first night in my flat, engrossed in a Koontz novel and just happened to look up. Don't know why I looked up or if something had caught my eye and then I saw it. It was only about an inch or so across and was directly above my head. It looked like a small spider with a couple of broken legs. I am afraid of spiders but not like phobia afraid, just enough sense to know not to pick them up. Many years ago as a child I saw a close up poster of a hairy spider with half a dozen eyes and huge poisonous fangs that would drop an elephant.

The poster gave me nightmare that was so real I can still recall it in vivid detail.

The crack was just a tiny crack and I remember smiling to myself as I walked across the bedroom and turned off the light. For some strange reason the crack amused me as I recalled the nightmare for what it was. A boy's childish dream being chased around a room by a spider and a witch. A man sized spider with a face like the poster and a cackling witch with pink and black socks. The archetypical witch in folklore and oz.

It was a few days later that a noise woke me. I couldn't quite put my finger on what it was or where it had come from. The noise was gone before I had time to rouse myself properly. I looked around the bedroom taking in the deep silent shadows while listening intently. I could hear the occasional car passing down Heaton Road which was a couple streets away, but silence, a thick heavy silence was in the room with me. A sombre threatening silence. There had been a noise I was sure of it and then I realised that I was sweating profusely. My clock said 3.35.

I needed a pee but I was afraid. Sounds stupid a grown man afraid to get up during the night but I felt there was something wrong. Something was watching me like a spider would watch a fly hoping it would land on her web. Just a weird horrible feeling that overcame my rational mind. I think I lay like that for about ten minutes then I just had to go, I had to piss. With a loud yawn I steeled myself and then just took a deep breath and got up. I needed the toilet but I was afraid. Sounds stupid a grown man afraid to get up during the night but I felt there was something wrong. Something was watching me like a spider would watch a fly hoping it would land on her web. Just a weird horrible feeling that overcame my rational mind. I lay like that for nearly twenty minutes then I just had to go, I had to piss. I was bursting. With an extraordinarily loud yawn I steeled myself then a deep breath and got up. My heart was pounding. Nothing bit or attacked me. Nothing took my soul or jumped into my body. Just a feeling and a noise that had really unsettled me. I got back into bed and before I turned on my side (I usually sleep in the curled foetus) just happened to look at the little spider who had grown an extra two legs. I was tired and really didn't give it a second thought. I was being stupid.

Up for work at dawn and never gave spidey a glance. Just flicked off the light and crawled into bed for a few days. It was three times the size and the long legs (there were eight now) had what looked like small hairs sprouting.

The crack was getting bigger. The spider was getting bigger and more intimidating. It was going to visit my dreams, I just knew it. I happened to be in town browsing through the Grainger market when I came across a shop selling kaftans and wolf pictures and dream catchers. It was a spur of the moment purchase. It was large with a grey timber wolf and a red Indian embossed around the web, and two white feathers; It might sound stupid but when I was talking to the young girl (wore a kaftan with a white wolf emblazoned) who sold it to me she swore they worked. They catch and trap the bad dreams before they reach you.

I pinned it to the wall above my headboard.

It worked. Although I slept well and woke up for a piss during the night, I kept thinking I could hear the spider-thing hissing and groaning. I consciously avoided looking at the crack because it scared me. I knew it was an irrational fear but scared is scared.

Another week passed and it was the size of one of those huge coconut eating crabs that I had seen on an Attenborough programme. Same shape. Same huge grasping claws and beady eyes. It was getting ready to eat me. Ready to step from the ceiling and devour me, popping my skull like a hairy coconut. Maybe I watch too much TV.

I awoke needing a piss and heard the creature creak as it stretched its legs that went all the way across the ceiling. I needed a wee sooo badly. The spider dared me to get out of bed. It moaned and screeched.

I needed to go, the pain was unbearable like a stabbing cramp in the lower half of my stomach. There was nothing else for it. I had to move. My heart was banging so hard I could hear it and feel my temples throbbing in time with the beat. When you gotta go.....In one movement I threw back the covers and dived out of bed. "Noooo." I screamed as loud as my trembling voice allowed and I kept low, kept my head bowed away from those deadly pincers and ran into the bathroom. I jerked on the pull cord that lit the room and then it happened.

A loud screech followed by a creak then a huge bang.

My bedroom ceiling had fell in.

I pissed myself.

My uncle Theodore was laying out the table for our tea. He was humming. He usually did this when deep in thought. After a few moments of listening to his unrecognisable tune I waited patiently for him to speak. "I might be leaving you soon". He said bluntly. "There is no easier way to say it cept by saying it as it is."

I looked up quickly from the superman comic I was reading. I didn't speak but gave him a questioning look with lowered eyebrows. He had spoken quickly and I knew he hadn't meant to say it or blurt it out like that because he went very quiet.

Was he waiting for me to speak? I didn't, couldn't.

He sighed and continued putting the cutlery on the plain white table cloth. It was a long time before he spoke. "I wanted to be here longer but am getting itchy feet again. You know young skywalker, I have been to many places and seen so much... I have danced the sun dance with the Navaho Indians and integrated myself into several tribes deep in the Amazonian jungle. In darkest Africa I was chased by cannibal pygmies. It took two days to lose them. I almost married a tribal king's daughter too but that's another story." He paused for a few moments a thin smile on his face reminiscing. He cleared his throat. "I have been here five months now and I have only stayed this long because I have enjoyed your company. Life is an adventure and laying on the sofa with the remote just isn't me." There was a slight almost imperceptible tremor in his voice. "I had expected to settle down here but my feet are getting itchy again and there are so many places yet to see. I have a bucket list as long as your arm to complete before I die."

I had a lump in my throat and swallowed hard. "When?"

Uncle Theodore stroked his chin thoughtfully. "It will take a long time to organise. Things to do, bags to pack and flights to sort etc. Possibly a month. Maybe two."

My heart sank. We ate our casserole in silence. I could think of nothing to say.

Did you know, have you yet realised that when you wake up at 3 or maybe 4 am for no apparent reason, there is a very good possibility that something or someone is staring at you from the shadows. Watching. Waiting.

What is a baby smiling and talking to when there is nothing there? Just because your senses cannot pick it up doesn't mean it is not watching you. And it is there!!!

A FORGOTTEN LOVE

You stroke his soft head
Gently, gently,
Put him back in his nice warn bed,
Gently, gently.
A pup, new born, helpless, blind,
Tender loving thoughts
Creep into your mind,
Gently, gently.
Cries only once and then lies still,
Bury him under a willow tree,
Make a stick cross, for all to see,
Gently, gently.
The years go by the cross falls,
Grass covers all.
You have forgotten him,
But he was so small,
Why was he ever born at all?

My Uncle Theodore told me many stories and little anecdotes during the six months he shared my life. He was always coming out with them but he actually told me very little about his travels into the deep jungles of Borneo and Tanzania and Brazil among many others. If I asked him he would reply with a sentence or two but he would never elaborate or go into details. I never thought it strange at the time, but upon reflection, it was really weird because he loved talking. I stayed with him because of the stories and I suppose it was because he treated me like an adult. My parents still treated me like a child; they talked down to me, but they were teachers so I guess it comes with the territory.

The stories he told engrossed me and so looked forward to them because they really happened. He said they did and I believed him, why wouldn't I? He was my long lost Uncle Theodore and I loved him. Not in a sexual way or anything like that just like a relative who I bonded with and enjoyed his company.

"This story happened a long time ago before your grandparents were even born." Uncle Theodore sipped on his hot chocolate and sat back in his big orange corduroy armchair. I settled opposite him on the matching sofa, put my feet up and closed my eyes. It was getting cold and the dark nights were closing in. It was going to be a long winter. My Unc paused for a few moments before he spoke in his deep rich voice.

THE LEGEND OF JOHN AND GILLIAN

"They were a really happy family until their father developed a cough and within a month he was dead of pneumonia. The tiniest of gods creations, thousands could fit comfortably on the eye of a needle, took down a healthy powerful giant of a man. The family buried him in the vegetable garden themselves. A small cross and a knee high picket wooden fence marked the grave.

They were poor now that father was gone. The man of the house left little for his family. John was only ten and his sister Gillian Levy was eight. Their mother was a sickly woman with consumption or tuberculosis as it is known today. John ran errands and did everything possible to keep a roof above their heads but after a harsh winter they had to move out of their house and into a rundown thatched cottage that also sheltered a family of rats and a multitude of insects. The biting bedbugs kept them awake at night. Crawling scuttling filthy mites that fed on their blood and then crawled into holes and spaces when the cock crowed to digest their meal. The floor covering was dirty straw and mud and dirt lined the walls.

The farmer had been a good friend of their fathers and he did not charge them rent for the cottage and although John and Gillian worked for him he paid them only with food. He gave them meat once a week as a treat. They them meat once a week as a treat. They retrieved water from the nearby stream and boiled it. The hours were long but not really physically hard. The farmer had a couple of hands working for him and they did most of the toil. Gillian ran his errands and kept his house clean.

It was a warm dry summer one of the driest on record. (Although I don't really think records were kept then). John got back one evening as usual. He picked up a well-used dented tin cup and went to the bucket for the water.

"I am sorry John, I wasn't too well today. I just didn't have the energy to get out of bed and get to the stream. I have had several of those hacking coughs that are followed by dizzy spells. There is stew in the pot if you are hungry. Can you bring me some water please? This Consumption makes my throat so dry." Mama's voice was rough and raspy.

Today was one of her bad days. She had one or two a month now. They were becoming more frequent. She lay on the floor with the coarse blanket pulled up to her chin and John could see the beads of sweat glistening on her forehead. Her head was turned to face him. "Can you take Gillian with you?" She didn't like her daughter to see the violent coughing fits. Each fit shortened her life. Everyone knew that.

John closed his eyes and nodded and picked up the metal bucket. "I will eat later mam." his smile was forced. There was always food in the pot. Plenty of food and nothing else.

It wasn't far to the stream. They walked along the well-trodden pathway lined on either side with trees and then up a small hillock and the stream was there then it flowed away from the cottage around a bend and on to the village about two miles away.

There was no stream. A thick gooey mud confronted them. The water had dried up. Gillian grabbed her brother's arm. "What's happened?" She was afraid.

"I dunno little sis but we are going to have go to where the water is coming out. Mother has to have it and I need a good wash." His mouth was dry but he didn't mention it.

"So we just got to keep looking then?" She looked up at her brother expectantly.

"Well either that or we all go thirsty and mam... mam needs it Gillian."

The pathway ended and Gillian held her brothers hand as they walked through deep grass that went over her knees as they walked to one side of the stream. Dirty hands held tight. They were nervous, the children had never been this far from home. Uncharted land. The mud was quickly drying. There was a raised bank on either side they tentatively walked along this then John stopped after a while. "We gotta go on, we don't have much choice." John looked up. "I want you to stay here its dangerous and gets very steep."

"No I am coming with you." Gillian squeezed his hand. She had an obstinate streak and John couldn't be bothered to argue. He was tired and his mouth was dry, he flicked his tongue over his lips to try and moisten them.

They didn't talk as they climbed. The grassy bank was replaced by rock. The steep hill became a climb. John slipped on the mossy hill and almost fell. "Gillian I think we had better turn back. This is getting too dangerous."

She nodded. She was nine years old and had been crying silently after grazing her ankle on a sharp rock. It was bleeding.

They turned. The moss was slippy and they fell. John dropped the bucket and tried to grab his sister but she was wrenched from his grasp. She screamed.

It wasn't a long fall but they did hit a few rocky outcrops on the way. Jack hit his head and a heavy blackness overcame him. We don't know how long he was out for but when he came around he looked for his little sis. His head was pouring with blood and he had to wipe it from his eyes several times as he called for Gillian.

He found her eventually at the foot of the hill. She was very small and very light and she was lying with her eyes open fixed staring ahead but there was no light left in them. Her neck was broken. He cradled her in his arms screaming her name...Gillian... Gill...Gill...

Up Jack got and home did trot as fast as he could caper.

He went to bed to mend his head with vinegar and brown paper…

Uncle Theodore left after telling me a couple more tales on his last night in the bungalow. It was the saddest night of my life up to that point. In an attempt to lighten my mood and raise my spirits he showed me a large S shaped scar on his thigh where he said an arrow had pierced and a straight scar on his right shoulder about four inches long where a spear had caught him. Uncs said he had to kill a man with his bare hands. A life or death situation, he had strangled the life out of the painted African tribal warrior who my Uncle said wore a scary carved wooden painted mask.

THE NUT TREE

Stannington is on the outskirts of Morpeth, Northumberland, about thirteen miles from Newcastle upon Tyne. A small quaint village where everyone knew everyone else's business and now it was expanding. The house we moved into was newly built upon on the derelict site of a mental hospital called St Mary's.

Apparently St Mary's sanatorium had housed some of the craziest and evil vagabonds ever to walk this country and some of the houses and flats were built into the hospital because of the listed buildings, but ours wasn't. Thank fuck. It was very close to the buildings but at least it wasn't in the large complexes. St Mary's asylum covered over one hundred acres and the new build estate was still expanding and most of it was still a bustling construction site. I had little to do during the holidays except explore the village and the surrounding land. There was mam and dad and my little brother Joe. I am Geoff by the way. Geoffrey Lance Hill, and I am fourteen.

One day after we had been there a few weeks I decided to cross the great expanse of grassland that would soon to be built upon. I came across a dry stone wall that I had to climb over, then a steep slope full of long grass and wild blackberry bushes that went on for forty yards or so that led to another higher dry stone wall. It couldn't be seen because of the thorny bushes that I had navigated with barely a scratch. This wall was taller than a man and I climbed it to look upon an orchard and a quaint little cottage that had grey smoke coming from the chimney even though it was the end of summer it was still quite warm. I had never seen anything like it in my life. There was a well-tended lawn and among this stood four trees. They weren't particularly large or imposing as trees go, but they did have the best looking fruit I have ever seen.

There was a pear tree and the pears were so large that the branches of that tree bent with the weight. An apple tree with the reddest of apples, a cherry tree with so many cherries you could barely see the leaves and a tree of fat purple plums with the juice oozing onto the grass.

I had my feet comfortably wedged into a gap and only my head could be seen peering over the wall which I guess was about seven or eight feet high. I took in the orchard and the cottage with its cracked and peeling window panes and green flaking door with barely any

Paint left on. The windows had never been cleaned -forever- by the looks of them. This was the back door because I could see a narrow lane passing along the front of the cottage. Wide enough for a car but not two.

Then I heard her singing. I had not seen the door open and I just managed to duck my head out of sight and gave a slight gasp with surprise.

But I had to look. Wouldn't you? I hesitantly peeped over the wall.

I spy with my little eye.

One couldn't guess her age from this distance. She could have been forty or eighty, with long very thin wispy ginger hair. She wore a plain long brown skirt that covered her feet and a white buttoned blouse that was opened at the neck. Over the blouse and around her neck, she wore like a lord mayor's chain, the biggest well... sparkliest gold necklace I have ever seen. It glinted and twinkled in the sunlight reflecting like a mirror. There was a silver something at the end and I am pretty sure it was a huge diamond, not that I had ever seen one. I just knew.

She stopped her singing and spoke to no one in particular because there was no one there. "It's going to be nice today I think. The sun is shining and I smell..." she paused and appeared to be sniffing the air, "fruit trees. Happy fruit trees." I crouched even lower. Maybe an old St Marys inmate. The thought came and I dismissed it quickly. The hospital had been derelict now for about twenty years.

She began waving her arms around in a purposeful way. A well-rehearsed dance. The necklace reflected and glinted with her movements and I was transfixed, almost mesmerised by the flashing diamond.

My foot slipped and I fell back and took a little skin off my knuckles and whacked my knee against a stone. I gritted my teeth against the pain. That was going to bruise tomorrow. After a few moments of gathering my composure I climbed back up the wall to peek over. The lady was coming out of the house through the back door and was pulling a brown thick woollen shawl onto her shoulders that matched her skirt. I noticed that her shimmering gold necklace was gone.

She was mumbling to herself but in a clear voice she said, "I have to get some shopping now. Am like old mother Hubbard whose cupboard was bare." She closed the back door went around to the front of the house and set off down the lane, the shops were about two miles away and she used a walking cane.

The ginger haired woman had closed the door but hadn't locked it. Usually I wouldn't notice anything like that but I did this time. I guess that in this isolated old cottage you would not really need to. What were the chances of someone happening along a country lane in the middle of nowhere then happening to knock on the door and then happening to enter if there was no answer?

Answers on a postcard please.

I am a fourteen year old boy. I had seen her leave and knew she had left the necklace behind and I wanted to see it close up. I had no intention of stealing it so wasn't really up to mischief, I just wanted a look. I was just inquisitive. I have never stolen anything in my life.

After taking one quick glance around I climbed over the wall, which was harder than it looked, and jumped the last few feet. My knee was still stinging but I tried to ignore it and I crouched down to look and listen.

There wasn't a single breeze but I could see the branches of the fruit trees gently waving and making the very green leaves dance.

Keeping low I skirted around the trees toward the farmhouse.

It really was an amazing garden, everything so colourful and well... Beautiful. That's not a word an ordinary fourteen year old would use but it's the only word I can find to describe it. Magical, like the colours straight out of the merry old Land of Oz

Near the door of the house hidden by the other trees, there was a smaller but more elegant one I had only seen in books. A nutmeg tree.

We had done a science project where we had to pick a tree and write an essay. I chose the nutmeg tree. I don't know why. Just wanted to do a different tree to the rest of the class. I got my first and only A plus for it. Took me a week and I was the last to hand in the essay.

There have been wars fought over the nutmeg tree which the Dutch won and then enslaved the people, and controlled the East Indies until the Second World War. The fruit is yellow with red and green marks and it resembles a large apricot. They grow to about 65 feet although this one was barely six and the colourings on it were amazing.

As I stood and looked at it the tips of the lower branches trembled in the still air. Eventually I had to take a deep breath and consciously turn away from the well-trimmed tree to the door. I could have gazed at the nutmeg tree for hours. I had seen pictures and drew a leaf and tree for my essay but I had never seen one in the flesh. Then I didn't hesitate, could not. My heart was pounding and palms were sweating as I strode toward the door and turned the well-polished brass knob without pausing. It was uncomfortably warm to the touch, and I pushed the green door wide open with my arm outstretched.

It wasn't at all like I expected. It certainly didn't look like that from the outside. It wasn't dull, dreary and dark, it was exactly the opposite. Bright, light and airy and very large with beautiful furniture and a thick red carpet. Weird.

The back door lead straight into the living room and I was taken aback at how modern it was with several pressed flowers in black frames on a white wall and a white three piece that I think was leather. A large picture of a smiling flame haired boy about my age was above the fireplace with a small bunch of purple flowers hanging from the corner. A small copper bowl was suspended above the fire on a hooked rod, it held something that bubbled gently and was lime green in colour. I just assumed at the time it was green tea because my mam sometimes drank it and that's what it looked like. Strange why the old woman would use the fireplace though when she could easily use a kettle in the kitchen.

Then I saw it. There was the necklace lying on a small occasional table carved in the image of a trumpeting elephant, it was in a far corner of the room beside the white leather sofa. I went across and picked it up. The thing that had sparkled and twinkled in the sunlight wasn't a full proper diamond. It was a gold circle with a diamond in the shape of an eye in the centre with some wording around it in a foreign language. It was amazing to look at. I was mesmerised by its beauty and it felt so old. I said the foreign words aloud as I caressed the eye with my fingers. They cried out to be read. You could not handle the necklace and not say the words. They stood out in bold tiny diamond lettering on the gold band.

I wasn't going to steal it but I made my way to the back door holding it like the crown jewels although it was incredibly light and cool to the touch. I have never stolen anything in my life I just wanted to see it sparkle in the sunlight again.

I was in the garden...

There was no dizziness or fainting or bangs or anything, there was just...just nothing, a blackness. When I came around I felt strange and disoriented. The strange woman was standing a few feet away from me holding a spade and wearing the necklace.

Up close she was old and painfully thin and I took an instant dislike to her sneering smug, self-satisfied, weather-beaten face. There were large dark circles under her eyes that reminded me of a giant panda. She had a blue headscarf over her head that tied under her chin.

"Well now how do you feel?" her voice was harsh, cracked and there was no emotion in it.

I couldn't talk, couldn't move. I was frozen to the spot.

"This is what happens to sneaky slimy thieves. My garden is full of them. Even my own son, my only child who I loved so much. I planted him beside the door, you may have seen him on your way into my house you sneaky sneak. I get some lovely flowers from him."

I tried to move. I was rigid. This was getting weird and scary. The only thing I could move were the tips of my fingers and even then they felt heavy, strange.

A blue bottle fly alighted on my face and I could feel its feet beating a pattern as it walked across what should have been my eyebrow. I still had feeling, rather acute feeling too, like my nerves had been heightened.

"You will turn back eventually although not for some years." She smiled a weak thin lipped smile. "But I can expect some nice lemons from you; but first I have to prune you down quite a bit." She picked up a pair of shears from the ground just out of my line of sight.

My fingertips waved like crazy.

My name is Geoffrey Lance Hill and I am fourteen.

THE PRINCE

He didn't know about vampires, didn't even know they existed until he was bitten.

He was young, tall, tanned and handsome, full of exuberance and vitality as only a twenty two year old can be.

She came to him one night and chose him from a small group of travelling warriors.

Her name? Well she has had many over the thousands of years since she was born, but for now, at this time she was Arcadia. For many years they had lived side by side with mankind, using them, feeding upon the weak and sick until a revelation and mankind hit back. Now as far as she knew, she was the last of her kind.

Her teeth were so sharp he didn't feel them pierce his jugular. He didn't feel her hand push his head back and with the other pin his two hands together on his chest.

It was only then he awoke and attempted to struggle and squirm.

Arcadia felt the blood rushing into her mouth and greedily she drank, the blood lust now at its peak. She could feel his strong heart beating, hear the blood rushing through his veins, hear his lungs sucking in air. She could also sense his cruelty toward fellow man and the corruption of his soul. He was unwashed and unkempt, a soldier of fortune who took the spoils of war and had thrust his sword into the backs of many, some for the smallest of sleights.

This one was strong, strong as an ox and Arcadia had never felt such a rush, so powerful, so orgasmic. She had sucked the blood of a thousand men, more uncountable children, babes, women all were quarry to be hunted. She did not feed every night or every week but once a month like a cold blooded reptile.

This man would have to be "made," A long torturous process where they usually died in absolute agony and could not be brought back. She had tried it many times before but all attempts had failed. She knew instinctively it could be done and how to do it but they invariably died screaming with their blood boiling and their veins popping with little cracking noises.

His name we still know and many fear, although Arcadia's final demise is lost in the mists of time.

Count Dracula still lives and he could be residing in your neighbourhood right now and could be working night shift.

He has intelligence way beyond our own and a cunningness developed over five hundred years of self preservation.

Possibly a security guard or some other night worker.

THE BICYCLE

"Mam tell him..."
"It's mine..."
"No, its mine..."

Jen dried her hands on the dish towel quickly. This was getting ridiculous. As she entered the sitting room she saw her two sons arguing over the bike. It was only an old blue bike with chipped paint and rusting handlebars but they fought tooth and nail over it. Gary aged ten had hold of the seat and Philip who was eleven was pulling on the front wheel.

Jen went over and picked up the bike. "Right that's enough, if you can't play together am putting it back in the hall." As she wheeled the bike out of the room she said "Santa comes in two days and you have to be good. Best behaviour."

Jennifer Lyttle was stressed. Her husband had walked out almost a year ago and she was finding it so hard to bring up the children alone. They were always needing new clothes and she could barely afford the food and bills and now Christmas. This was going to be the best

ever. Jen had saved and scrimped and even took on a part time job while the children were at school. It was all down to her now. Everything was down to her since he had left. The children were quite well behaved except where the bicycle was concerned and then they fought and argued through clenched teeth.

A neighbour had bought a new one for her son and gave the old one to Jen some three months ago for Philip. He was the taller of the two and it was his size.

Philip Lyttle was the shy one and quite subdued. He was ill on a regular basis, if any bug went around he would get it and end up in hospital. His immune system wasn't too good, didn't work as it should have and several pills and an injection a day kept the worst bugs away. He was painfully thin with an unruly mop of blonde hair.

Gary was more boisterous and adventurous. He was always playing tricks, getting into scrapes and a staunch defender of his brother. Woe betide anyone who said a bad word or deed against

Philip. Although not alike they were clearly brothers and shared the mop of shaggy blonde hair.

Where the bicycle was concerned though they were sworn enemies and it could not be shared.

Love forgotten to be replaced by sibling rivalry over an old bike with a bell that had surface rust and a creaking ping.

Jen had tried everything to stop the arguments that commenced every night after school that continued through the winter holidays. She had been at different times, exasperated, angry and depressed. As a single parent the boys were her life. Their happiness made her happy but they could be trying at times.

Christmas Eve.

"Come on guys, bedtime. Jen Lyttle smiled. For the first time in a long while no arguments or disagreements over the blue bike. They had been bathed and had their onesies on. Gary, an army camouflage and Philip a giraffe. They climbed into their beds at either side of the room. "How are you feeling Philip?" She asked her son kissing him on the cheek.

"Not too well mam. Feel a bit sick actually."

"Well you have had all your pills and medicines for today but if you get any worse come and wake me up okay babe."

He nodded and she kissed him again on the forehead. Gary had been watching and he said "I want two kisses too mam. Not fair if I only get one "

Jen laughed. She was happy. For the first time in such a long time her laugh wasn't forced.

Christmas Day.

Gary ran into his mams room. "Mam quick, hurry."

"What…whatsup. What." Sleep fought to hold on to her.

"Quickly. Mam move." He grabbed her arm at the wrist and pulled.

"Okay kay am up." Still struggling with sleep she sat up. Gary pulled at her wrist.

"Mammy please…"

She got up and without pulling a dressing gown over her PJs went out the bedroom door and into the sitting room with Gary leading her by the hand.

She stopped. Froze. There was the blue bicycle cycling around the sitting room in tight circles. She watched it go around twice slowly then the bell with its surface rust pinged twice as the cycle went through the open door and into the hallway. It stopped, fell against the wall and never moved again.

Jen Knew she had closed the hallway door and she just watched the bike with her hands clapped to her cheeks in shock and surprise.

Gary wrote a note to put in his brothers coffin it read:

"I love you so much and miss you more than words can say. It was always your bike and I was stupid and jealous. Philip please forgive me. Come back please I don't want to be alone. Love you my big brother."

He kissed the note with the most loving kiss he would ever give in his lifetime.

Philip had always been ill.

His presents now dusty have never been opened and along with his shiny new red bicycle still lie beneath the stairs. The fading Santa tag on it says; To Philip. Have a lovely Christmas my darling. Hope you like this new one. Have a fantastic Christmas my little man. xx

Goodbye Uncle Theodore. You said we will meet again but it has been twenty years now and in the back of my mind I think some tribe must have caught you and didn't understand your sign language. Maybe not. Maybe you will walk up and knock on my door one dark and rainy night...

The old doctor yawned and took off his gold coloured spectacles to rub his bloodshot eyes, he was counting the days down to his final retirement. He could have retired years ago but decided to stay on at St Mary's for three days a week. He had made a difference to people's lives and now eagerly looked forward to putting his feet up. Retirement seemed a good idea at this time in his life.

He sat hunched, elbows resting on a large desk, holding his spectacles by one gold arm. The polished desk held a laptop, a white desk lamp and several brown files. A modern day hospital yet it still used files alongside computers. They looked out of place on the desk.

He replaced his glasses after giving them a polish with a cloth from the pocket of his white work coat. "Time to see what the dayshift have been up to?" He spoke aloud. A ritual he had been doing for almost thirty years. He opened the top brown file after glancing at the name of the patient. He read the notes.

"Theodore Fish has been telling his stories again today. He still tells them to the young boy named Luke who we now know to have been thirteen year old Lucas Johnston. Theodore Fish was convicted of killing and eating the boy. He was his nephew. He speaks and behaves as though the boy was there in the cell with him.

We do know that he was involved in some way with all the stories he tells but although clinically insane he is also very devious. We do firmly believe, although cannot prove it yet and he will not admit to it, that he has killed and eaten several people after being introduced to it by a tribe of head-hunters in Borneo. (Yes they still exist.)

Theodore believes he is related to the notorious serial killer Albert Fish, although this may or may not be true, he was put in an orphanage at an early age.

When arrested Theodore had in his pocket a folded up typed article which was the confession of one Albert Fish I will include several lines just to put it into perspective.

Quote "I took four year old Billy Gaffney, gagged him with an old rag and whipped his bare behind till the blood ran. I cut off his ears and then his nose and slit his mouth from ear to ear. He died when I gouged out his eyes then I stuck the knife in his belly and drank his blood." Unquote.

"Theodore Fish is a very dangerous man and must remain in this asylum until his last breath."

The old Doctor closed the file.

Time for his pill. He had recently been diagnosed with dementia and it was time to retire. A retirement with no future.

He hoped he had made a difference.

BE A MAN

It was cold. Freezing in fact, and my breath in the still chill air was smoking dragon's breath.

I pulled up the collar on my thick woollen overcoat. Black over coat over a well cut black suit. Perfect funeral attire.

My name is Alan Jacobs, big Al to my friends. Bastard Al to my enemies. I stand at six four in my bare feet and am an electrician by trade. I recently lost my job through no fault of my own. The company I worked for tried to expand and fell flat on its ass. Ten years of my life, of sweat and sleepless nights; for what. A few hundred quid in the bank and fuck off thank you very much.

So through the loss of a job a house was lost.

I couldn't keep up the mortgage payments. We tried so hard, we really did but the bank (heartless bastards) took it from us. We were devastated. My wife and two children moved in with her parents and I moved in with my mam. I took to drinking quite heavily because it made me forget the bad things in my life. I didn't realise it at the time but the alcohol addled my brain so much that I also forgot the good things.

My wife said she spent most nights crying herself to sleep and I wasn't really in any state to comfort her. I viewed the world for a while through the bottom of a glass. We didn't see each other much although we were still married be it in name only.

It was left to a friend to tell me. They say you are always the last to know. She had her eyes on another man and obviously had stopped crying herself to sleep.

For the loss of a job the marriage was lost.

I had to confront her but I could have done it better. I went to the house not to cause trouble but to get to the root of the insinuations. Her dad answered the door and said she wasn't at home. When I asked to see my children he had to admit that they weren't there either. I don't think I was aggressive but I was angry and he told me that she lived a few streets away. We had been good friends in another life. He told me to behave and sober up "BE A MAN" The words bounced around in my head. BE A MAN.

I found the house but I was drunk and shouted in the street. I was nasty and abusive. I saw my two sons watching me from an upstairs window. "Come out lads and give your old man a hug." I didn't realise my words were slurred. I watched my wife, MY wife ushering the children away from the window. That's when I saw red and threw the wheelie bin through the living room window. I was arrested and apparently resisted arrest and banned with a court order from seeing my two sons and going near my wife.

For the loss of a job the family was lost.

Then my car was repossessed. It was just a family saloon in silver with all the bells and whistles and it was my pride and joy and just over two years old. I had nothing left.

I done some drugs and hit the drink hard. Numb. More drugs more drink. Numb. I wanted my home my wife, my children, my car, a job. A life. The drink and the drugs eased the pain and helped me forget what I lost.

So sad too bad your fucked.

For the loss of a job I had nothing.

A short stint in St Marys hospital to try and sort my head but then I signed myself out. Depression is a demon that gets in through your ears while you sleep and plays with your mind.

I am standing on the wide handrail of the Newcastle Tyne Bridge, dressed in my best funeral attire. I walked slowly along the newly painted green bridge but just before the fast flowing river Tyne took over, there was a long drop to the concrete and the road. I climbed the handrail.

I had lost everything and felt there was no reason to go on. Life was a burden I could no longer shoulder. What would you do?

For the loss of a job a life was lost.

BE A MAN.

I didn't jump or do a swallow dive or anything like that. I fastened the last button of on my over coat, took a deep breath and I simply leaned forward and closed my eyes.

The wind roared in my ears like a jet engine. My face felt so cold and I opened my eyes tears blurring my vision.

I didn't want to die.

END

Printed in Dunstable, United Kingdom

67725461R00030